KU-213-154

The Rainbow Book of Nursery Tales

Written and illustrated by

Sam Childs

RED FOX

Schools Library and Information Services

S00000671528

For David Jenkin,
my very own Prince Charming

DLEY PUBLIC LIBRARIES

L 47986

G71528 | SCH

J 398.2

THE RAINBOW BOOK OF NURSERY TALES
A RED FOX BOOK 0 09 943878 X

First published in Great Britain by Hutchinson,
an imprint of Random House Children's Books

Hutchinson edition published 2003
Red Fox edition published 2005

1 3 5 7 9 10 8 6 4 2

Copyright © Sam Childs, 2003

The right of Sam Childs to be identified as the author and illustrator of this work has
been asserted in accordance with the Copyright, Designs and Patents Act 1988.

All rights reserved. No part of this publication may be reproduced, stored in a retrieval system,
or transmitted in any form or by any means, electronic, mechanical, photocopying,
recording or otherwise, without the prior permission of the publishers.

Red Fox Books are published by Random House Children's Books,
61–63 Uxbridge Road, London W5 5SA,
a division of The Random House Group Ltd,
in Australia by Random House Australia (Pty) Ltd,
20 Alfred Street, Milsons Point, Sydney, NSW 2061, Australia,
in New Zealand by Random House New Zealand Ltd,
18 Poland Road, Glenfield, Auckland 10, New Zealand,
and in South Africa by Random House (Pty) Ltd,
Endulini, 5A Jubilee Road, Parktown 2193, South Africa

THE RANDOM HOUSE GROUP Limited Reg. No. 954009
www.kidsatrandomhouse.co.uk

A CIP catalogue record for this book is available from the British Library.

Printed in China

Contents

Foreword

by Sam Childs

What a delight! To be asked to compile and illustrate a book of nursery tales, which even the smallest children can enjoy. The challenge was to choose stories to suit this audience and then retell them in a friendly and accessible way. It has been a joy.

Folk and fairy tales evolved to help children to come to terms with and understand the world around them; they are full of universal truths. I am particularly fond of the ones where cunning or clever actions outwit the baddy! Take a look at *Stone Soup*, or one of my all-time favourites, *The Woman who Flummoxed the Fairies*.

Then we have cautionary tales like *Little Red Riding Hood*, *Goldilocks and the Three Bears* and *Little Lisa* – the children who pay no heed to their parents' good advice. They just can't resist straying and as a result have to deal with some pretty scary situations! And of course there is the irresistible magic of stories like *Cinderella*, *Sleeping Beauty*, *The Elves and the Shoemaker* and *The Frog Prince*.

These tales are full of recognizable characters. Some you love, some make you laugh, some you feel sorry for, and others just infuriate you! They have all been with us for hundreds of years and their message is as resonant today as it was when they were first told around the fireside. I hope you will find all your favourites here, and discover some lesser-known ones as well.

I can think of no better introduction to the wonders of storytelling than these much-loved tales. They are here for you to enjoy.

Boys and Girls

Little Red Riding Hood

There was once a little girl who lived with her mum and dad at the edge of a wood. Her dad was a woodcutter and worked in the wood all day long.

The little girl had a grandma who lived on the other side of the wood. She adored her little granddaughter and had sewed her a most beautiful cloak with a cosy hood, made out of red velvet.

The little girl loved her cloak and wore it all the time and soon people stopped calling her by her proper name – whatever that was – and started calling her Little Red Riding Hood.

One day her mum asked Red Riding Hood to take a basketful
of goodies to Grandma, who was not feeling well.
She had a bad cold and had tucked
herself up in bed. Little Red
Riding Hood put on her red
cloak, picked up the basket and
skipped off into the woods.

She hadn't gone far when she met a big grey wolf. She thought that he was a dog and a clever dog at that, because he spoke to her.

"Hello, little girl," he said. "Where are you off to on this bright sunny day?"

"I'm taking a basket of goodies to my grandma on the other side of the wood," she answered, "because she's in bed not well and needs cheering up."

"Why don't you pick some flowers for her too?" said the clever wolf.

Little Red Riding Hood thought that was a lovely idea, but as soon as she left the path to pick some flowers, the wolf bounded away as fast as he could to Grandma's cottage.

He knocked on the door and when Grandma asked who it was, he answered in a little squeaky voice, "It's me, Grandma, Little Red Riding Hood, with a big surprise for you."

"Well, lift up the latch and come in," called Grandma.

So the wolf opened the door, leapt across the room and swallowed Grandma with one great gulp. Then that sneaky wolf put on one of Grandma's nighties and tied on a bonnet to cover his enormous ears. He snuggled down in bed and pulled the covers up to hide as much of himself as he could.

Soon there was a knock on the door and the wolf asked who it was in a very croaky voice.

"It's me, Grandma, Little Red Riding Hood, with a basketful of goodies to cheer you up."

"Then lift up the latch and come in," called the wolf.

So Little Red Riding Hood opened the door and peered at Grandma in bed. Inside, the cottage was quite dark, especially after the bright sunshine outside, so Little Red Riding Hood couldn't see the wolf at all clearly.

"Oh, Grandma," she said, staring hard at her, "what big eyes you have."

"All the better to see you with, my dear," whispered the wolf.

"Oh, Grandma," she said, "what long arms you have."

"All the better to hug you with, my dear," said the wolf.

"Oh, Grandma," she said, "what big teeth you have."

"All the better to EAT YOU WITH," roared the wolf.

And he jumped out of bed and swallowed her with one gulp.

Now Little Red Riding Hood's dad had finished chopping wood for the day and he decided to go and see if Grandma was feeling any better, and then take Little Red Riding Hood home again.

When he arrived at the cottage, he found not Grandma, but the wolf in bed and with one sweep of his axe, he chopped off the wicked wolf's head and would you believe it, out jumped Grandma and Little Red Riding Hood, a little squashed looking, but none the worse for being eaten.

The woodcutter left Grandma with her basketful of goodies and her beautiful bunch of flowers and took Little Red Riding Hood safely home again.

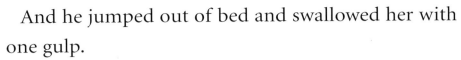

13

Goldilocks and the Three Bears

There was once a little girl called Goldilocks who always did what she shouldn't do.

One morning while her mummy and daddy were still fast asleep, she slipped out of the house and skipped off into the woods.

Now in a clearing in the trees there lived a family of bears. There was great big daddy bear, a middle-sized mummy bear and a little baby bear. That morning the daddy bear made a big pot of porridge and then ladled it into their bowls. But when they tasted it, it was hot, hot, HOT.

"Let's go for a walk while it cools down," said the middle-sized mummy bear, and off they went into the woods.

As Goldilocks was skipping through the woods, she saw the three bears' cottage and because she always did what she shouldn't do, she pushed the door open and went in. And what did she see on the table? Yes, three bowls of porridge. And because all that skipping had made her hungry, she scooped a spoonful of porridge from great big daddy bear's great big bowl.

"Ow," she cried. "Too hot!" So she scooped a spoonful from the middle-sized mummy bear's middle-sized bowl.

"Yuck," she cried. "Too cold!"

Then she scooped a spoonful from the little baby bear's little bowl.

"Mmmmm," she sighed. "This is just right."

And because she always did what she shouldn't do, she gobbled it all up.

All that skipping had made her tired, so she looked for a chair to sit on. First she sat on great big daddy bear's great big chair, but it was SO hard that it hurt her bottom. Then she jumped up and sat on middle-sized mummy bear's middle-sized chair, but it was so soft and squashy that she sank right in. So up she jumped and sat on little baby bear's little chair, which felt just right, but Goldilocks was much heavier than the little baby bear and, crack! the chair broke into pieces.

Then Goldilocks began to feel sleepy. And because she always did what she shouldn't do, she went upstairs into the three bears' big bedroom. First she climbed into great big daddy bear's great big bed, but it was so high that it made her feel dizzy. Next she climbed into middle-sized mummy bear's middle-sized bed, but it was too bouncy. Last she climbed into little baby bear's little bed, which was just right. So she snuggled down and went to sleep.

She was SO fast asleep that she didn't hear the three bears come back home for their breakfast. Great big daddy bear looked at his great big porridge bowl.

"Who's been eating my porridge?" he growled.

Middle-sized mummy bear looked at her middle-sized porridge bowl.

"And who's been eating my porridge?" she grumbled.

Little baby bear looked at his little porridge bowl.

"Who's been eating my porridge," he squeaked, "and gobbled it ALL UP?"

Then the three bears noticed their chairs.

"Who's been sitting on my great big chair?" growled great big daddy bear.

"Who's been sitting on my middle-sized chair?" grumbled middle-sized mummy bear.

"Who's been sitting on my little chair," squeaked little baby bear, "and broken it IN PIECES?"

The three bears climbed, clomp, clomp, clomp up the stairs to their bedroom.

"Who's been sleeping in my great big bed?" growled great big daddy bear.

"Who's been sleeping in my middle-sized bed?" grumbled middle-sized mummy bear.

"Who's been sleeping in my little bed," squeaked little baby bear, "and . . . and . . . IS STILL THERE!"

Great big daddy bear and middle-sized mummy bear hurried to little baby bear's bed, but too late!

Goldilocks leaped out of bed, through great big daddy bear's legs, round middle-sized mummy bear, down the stairs and out of the door. She ran and ran and ran as fast as she could back to her own house.

Luckily her mummy and daddy had only just woken up so they never knew that she had been out of the house. And, do you know? From that day on she hardly ever did what she shouldn't!

Lazy Jack

There was once a boy whose name was Jack. He lived with his mother and they were very poor. Jack's mother worked as hard as she could, but Jack just sat about, basking in the sun in summer and lazing by the fire in winter. And do you know, that was all he did, so it's not surprising that everyone who knew him called him Lazy Jack.

One Monday his mother decided that enough was enough.

"Jack, my boy," she said, "get up, get out, and get a job. If you don't bring back something to pay for your food, then you'll have to go hungry."

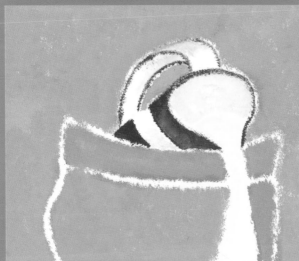

Jack was so shocked that he jumped up and got a day's work with the farmer next door. The farmer gave him a silver coin to take home, but Jack, who had never had any money before, accidentally dropped it into the river as he went over the bridge.

"Stupid boy!" cried his mother. "You should have put it in your pocket."

"I'll do that next time," said Lazy Jack.

On Tuesday Jack did a day's work for a cowman, who gave him a jug of milk to take home. Jack put it into his pocket, but by the time he got home, it was all spilled (and his trousers were soggy).

"Stupid, stupid, stupid boy!" said his mum. "You should have carried it on your head."

"I'll do that next time," said Lazy Jack.

On Wednesday Jack did a day's work for the farmer again.

This time the farmer gave him a big round cheese to take home.

Jack put the cheese on his head, but by the time he got home, half of it had melted and trickled down his neck, and birds had pecked at the rest.

"You silly, silly, silly boy," said his mum. "You should have carried it carefully in your hands."

"I'll do that next time," said Jack.

On Thursday Lazy Jack did a day's work for a baker, who gave him a large tomcat to take home.

Jack carefully carried the cat in his hands, but it scratched him so badly that he had to let it go.

"Stupid, stupid, stupid, stupid boy," cried his mother. "You should have put it on a lead and led it home."

"I'll do that next time," said Jack.

On Friday Jack did a day's work for a butcher, who gave him a leg of mutton to take home.

Jack put a lead on it and dragged it home behind him.

By the time he got home, most of the neighbours' dogs had had a good meal from it and what was left was covered in dirt.

"Stupid, stupid, stupid, stupid, STUPID boy!" cried his mother. "You should have carried it over your shoulder."

"I'll do that next time," said Jack.

On Saturday Lazy Jack did a day's work for a cattle keeper, who gave him a donkey to take home.

Poor Jack, he had a terrible time hoisting the donkey onto his shoulders and he nearly crumbled under its weight as he stumbled home.

On his way home he passed the house of a rich man, who lived with his beautiful daughter.

The poor girl never spoke and never laughed, but doctors said that she would speak if only somebody could make her laugh.

Now it happened that she was looking out of her window as Lazy Jack staggered and lurched past with the great big donkey on his shoulders. As soon as she saw him she burst into a great fit of laughter and shouted, "Bring that boy to me!"

Her father was so delighted to hear his daughter speak and laugh that he let her marry Jack. This meant that Jack became a rich man, so he was able to give his mother enough money to live comfortably for the rest of her life AND it meant that Jack never had to work again, which was just as well!

Little Lisa

There was once a little girl called Lisa, who lived with her mum and dad in a little red house.

On her birthday, her mum made her a beautiful orange dress. Lisa put it on with a pink and white striped apron and a bright blue scarf. Her dad bought her a pair of pretty purple shoes, a straw hat covered in flowers, a pair of little pink gloves and a beautiful parasol.

Lisa loved her new things and when she had put them all on, her mum said, "Here are six pennies. Now go to the village and buy some candles for your birthday cake. But make sure that you stay on the road and don't stray."

Lisa skipped off down the road. She had promised her mum that she would not leave it. But soon she saw some delicious wild strawberries in the bushes and began to eat them. The further into the bushes she went, the bigger the strawberries grew. Soon she was quite lost.

Just then she heard a deep growling sound,

"GRRRRR!"

And out in front of her lumbered a big brown bear.

"Yum!" he cried. "It's little Lisa. I think that I shall eat her all up!"

"Oh please don't eat me up, kind Mr Bear," she cried. "If you don't, I'll give you my pretty pink and white striped apron and my bright blue scarf."

"Oh, all right," said the big brown bear, and he tied the apron around his waist and the scarf around his head.

"Mmmm," he said, "I'm the most handsome creature in all the land."

29

Poor little Lisa went on her way but she had no idea how to find the road again. As she turned a corner she heard a horrible howl.

Out jumped a wild woolly wolf.

"Yum, yum!" he cried. "It's little Lisa. I think that I shall eat her all up."

"Oh please don't eat me up, kind Mr Wolf," she cried. "If you don't, I'll give you my lovely flowery hat and my pretty pink gloves."

"Oh, all right," said the wild woolly wolf. And he tied the hat under his hairy chin, and pulled the pink gloves onto his paws.

"Mmmm," he said, "I'm the most handsome creature in all the land."

Lisa set off on her way again. Suddenly she heard a sharp barking noise.

Out of the wood came a ferocious fox.

"Yum, yum, yum!" he said. "It's little Lisa, I think that I shall eat her all up."

"Oh please don't eat me up, kind Mr Fox," she cried. "If you don't, I'll give you my pretty parasol."

"Oh, all right," said the ferocious fox. And he twirled the parasol over his shoulder.

"Mmmm," he said, "I'm the most handsome creature in all the land."

Poor little Lisa. All that she had left was her orange dress and her little purple shoes. She was lost in the woods and the stars were already coming out.

Suddenly a little voice from nearby said, "Hello, little Lisa, you look lost. Can I help you at all?"

And a bob-tailed rabbit appeared in front of her.

"Oh, kind Mr Rabbit," she said, "I'll give you my best purple shoes if you show me the way back to the road."

"How wonderful!" said the bob-tailed rabbit. "Those will help me to run really fast. Hop onto my back and we'll reach the road in a twinkling."

Rabbit ran like the wind. Suddenly they heard the most terrible noise.

"Hold tight, little Lisa," whispered the rabbit, "and we'll peep round this tree to see who is making SUCH a din."

And what do you think they saw? The big brown bear, the wild woolly wolf and the ferocious fox all quarrelling over which of them was the most handsome.

Bear pushed wolf, wolf shoved fox, fox grabbed bear's tail, bear grabbed wolf's tail and wolf grabbed fox's tail. Round and round they chased each other, faster and faster until . . . first bear's apron and scarf flew off, then wolf's flowery hat and gloves fell to the ground, and finally fox's parasol whirled into the air.

They were so busy fighting that they didn't notice little Lisa picking up her clothes. When she had put them all back on, she tucked the parasol under her arm and jumped on the rabbit's back. The bob-tailed rabbit ran as fast as the wind, back to Lisa's house where her mum, because it was Lisa's birthday, made them waffles and jam. Little Lisa ate one hundred and thirty-three.

Can you believe it?

On the
Farm

The Little Red Hen

Once upon a time there was a little red hen. One day when she was out in her garden with her dear little chicks, she found some ears of wheat. Instead of eating them, she decided to plant them.

"Look!" she cried. "Lots of ears of wheat, who will help me to plant them?"

"Too tired," sighed the dozy dog.

"Too boring," whinged the crafty cat.

"Too busy," gurgled the wallowing pig.

So the little red hen shrugged and said, "Very well then, I'll plant them myself."

She dug the ground and raked it evenly and planted the grains of wheat in neat little rows.

Then she watered them every day until she had a lovely patch of golden wheat waiting to be cut.

"Look!" she cried. "The wheat is ripe, who will help me to harvest it?"

"Too tired," yawned the dozy dog.

"Too boring," yowled the crafty cat.

"Too busy," glugged the wallowing pig.

So the little red hen shrugged and said, "Very well then, I'll harvest it myself."

She got out her big scythe and cut the wheat. Then she took all the grains and put them in a big bag.

"Look!" she cried. "All the grain is in my big bag, who will help me to carry it to the miller to be made into flour?"

"Too tired," snored the dozy dog.

"Too boring," miaowed the crafty cat.

"Too busy," spluttered the wallowing pig.

So the little red hen shrugged and said, "Very well then, I'll carry it myself."

She hoisted the big bag on to a cart and, huffing and puffing, pulled it all the way to the mill, where the miller ground the golden grain into fine white flour.

Then the little red hen pulled her sack of flour all the way home again.

"Look!" she cried. "I am using my flour to bake with, who will help me to make a cake?"

"Too tired," mumbled the dozy dog.

"Too boring," moaned the crafty cat.

"Too busy," squelched the wallowing pig.

So the little red hen shrugged and said, "Very well then, I'll make it myself."

She mixed and beat and stirred no end of delicious things into her freshly ground flour and popped the cake into the oven.

As the caked baked a wonderful, mouth-watering smell wafted around the farm.

"Look!" said the little red hen finally. "My delicious cake is baked, who will help me to eat it?"

"Me, me, me!" barked the delighted dog.

"I will, I will!" purred the prancing cat.

"A big slice for me!" snorted the perky pig.

"Not a chance!" exclaimed
the little red hen. "You are all
too lazy and greedy."
    And she carried the cake right
past them and set it on a cloth
under the apple tree
where she and her
dear little chicks
ate it up – all
by themselves.

The Wolf and the Seven Little Kids

There was once an old mother goat who had seven little kids.
One day, as she got ready to go shopping, she said, "Kids, there's
a big bad wolf moved into the woods. Be sure
not to open the door to him if he knocks,
because he'll eat you for his dinner."

Their mother had not been gone long, when there was a knock on the door.

"Open up, my dear little kids," said a growly voice. "It's your mummy come home from the shops with lots of goodies for you."

"You're not our mum!" squeaked the littlest kid. "Our mum has a sweet soft voice, yours is all growly. GO AWAY!"

The wolf loped off to the chemist's shop. "Give me some throat sweets," he growled at the chemist, "or I'll eat you up."

Back he went to Mrs Goat's house and said in a much sweeter voice, "Open up, my gorgeous little kids, your mummy's home from the shops with seven strawberry lollies."

The littlest kid tried to peep through the keyhole, but all that he could see was a big paw on the door knocker.

"You're not our mum!" yelled the littlest kid. "You've got a great grey hairy paw. Our mum has dainty little white feet. GO AWAY!"

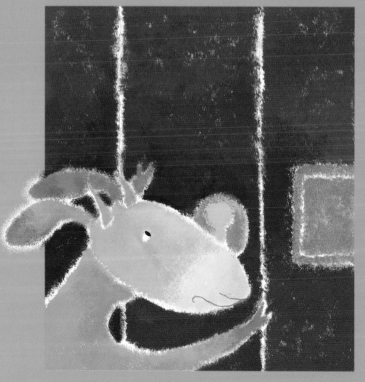
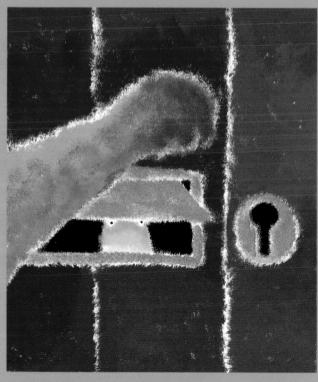

The wolf loped off to the mill. "Give me some flour to put on my paws or I'll eat you up," he growled at the miller.

The wolf wet his paws in the mill stream and dipped them into the bag of flour. Soon he had snowy white feet.

Back he went to Mrs Goat's house and said in a sweet voice, "Open the door, my darling wee kids. I've got crisps and orange juice for you. If you want to be sure that it's me, just look at my snowy white feet."

He pushed a paw through the letter-box and all the little kids cried, "It's our mum, back from shopping with presents for us!"

And they all ran to open the door. All except for the littlest kid, who hid in the bread bin, because he was not AT ALL sure that it was his mum at the door.

The wolf hurtled through the door and gobbled up the six little kids.

Then he set off home. He had not gone far when he needed a rest. Having six little kids in your tummy is very tiring. He sat down under a tree and fell fast asleep.

When Mrs Goat came home, she was shocked to find the door open and her darling little kids all gone.

She let out a loud scream, "AAARGH!"

At once the littlest kid jumped out of the bread bin and told her what had happened.

In no time at all Mrs Goat found the sleeping wolf and snipped open his tummy with a large pair of scissors. Out jumped one, two, three, four, five, SIX little kids.

She gave them all a kiss and then filled up the wolf's tummy with great big stones and stitched him up again.

When he woke up his tummy felt terrible. It was lumpy and bumpy and heavy – and it hurt.

"If eating kids makes me feel so TERRIBLE, I'll never do it again," he howled.

And do you know, he never did.

The Great Big Enormous Turnip

There were once an old husband and wife. They lived on a farm with a cow, two sheep, three hens, four geese and five pigs.

Every year, in the spring, they planted seeds to grow into vegetables for them to eat right through the year.

One year they planted peas, carrots, potatoes and turnips. But, DISASTER!

A mouse stole most of the peas. A rabbit ate most of the carrots. The potatoes were covered in black spots and the turnips were the size of radishes.

"Oh me, oh my," sighed the old man as he pulled up his turnips. "We have just enough food to see us through the summer, but whatever are we going to eat in the winter with no peas to dry, no carrots to store and turnips the size of radishes? We shall surely starve."

He had nearly come to the end of the row of turnips and started to pull out the last one, but it would not budge.

"Wife," he called, "please come and help me pull this turnip. It's stuck fast and won't budge."

So his wife put her arms around his waist and together they pulled. HEE, HA, HEE, HA. But the turnip would NOT be moved.

Then the old woman called to her cow, "Moo, please come and help us pull this turnip. It's stuck fast and won't budge."

So the cow took hold of the old woman, and together they pulled. HEE, HAW, HEE, HAW. But the turnip would NOT be moved.

The cow called the two sheep, "Baa and Baa, please come and help us to pull this turnip. It's stuck fast and won't budge."

So the sheep took hold of the cow and together they pulled. HEE, HUMPH, HEE, HUMPH. But the turnip would NOT be moved.

Then the sheep called the three hens, "Cluck, Cluck and Cluck, please come and help us to pull this turnip. It's stuck fast and won't budge."

So the hens took hold of
the sheep and together they pulled.

HEE, HO, HEE, HO.

But the turnip would NOT
be moved.

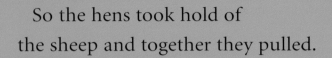

Then the hens
called the four geese,
"Gobble, Gobble, Gobble and
Gobble, please come and help us
to pull this turnip. It's stuck fast and won't budge."
So the geese took hold of the hens and together they pulled.

HEE, HUP, HEE, HUP.

But the turnip would not be moved. Then the geese
called the five pigs, "Honk, Honk, Honk, Honk and
Honk, please come and help us to pull this
turnip. It's stuck fast and won't budge."

So the pigs took hold of the geese and together they pulled.
HEE, HARUMPH, HEE, HARUMPH. But the turnip would
NOT be moved.

Sitting nearby was a little mouse. The very same mouse who
had eaten most of the peas that the old man and the old woman
had grown. He felt a bit sorry for them, so he squeaked,
"May I help too?"

"You!" said the old man.
"You!" said the old woman.
"You!" said the cow.
"You!" said the sheep.
"You!" said the hens.
"You!" said the geese.
"You!" said the pigs.
"YOU'RE TOO SMALL."

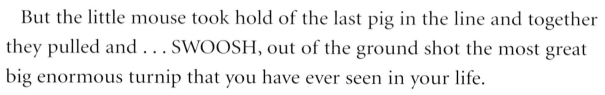

But the little mouse took hold of the last pig in the line and together they pulled and . . . SWOOSH, out of the ground shot the most great big enormous turnip that you have ever seen in your life.

And do you know, it fed the old man and the old woman for the whole of the winter. Wasn't that lucky for them!

Stone Soup

One day the Big Bad Wolf was out for a walk. He passed Mother Hen's house which looked very smart indeed, with its beautiful garden and smart new paintwork.

Hmmm, thought the Big Bad Wolf, I bet there are lots of nice things in that house. So he peered over the fence to see who lived there.

Mother Hen popped up from amongst her pumpkins.

"Greetings, Mother Hen," smiled the Big Bad Wolf. "I think that you would be perfect for my dinner. And when I've eaten you, I'll run away with all your lovely things."

"Oh, really?" said Mother Hen. "But if you are going to have a proper sit-down dinner you should start with soup. I shall make you some."

The wolf was delighted. Before he had time to decide WHICH soup to have, Mother Hen had picked up a large stone from the path.

"I'll make you stone soup," she said. Mother Hen popped the stone into a large pan of water and set it on the stove.

When it started boiling, she tasted it. "Salt and pepper!" she shouted.

The Big Bad Wolf handed them to her. She tasted it again.

"Carrots!" she said. "While I dig some up, just wash the dishes for me."

"OK," said the Big Bad Wolf, licking his lips.

Mother Hen came back and popped the carrots into the pan.

Then she took another taste.

"Onions!" she cried. "While I dig some up, just give the house a clean, would you?"

"OK," said the Big Bad Wolf, as his tummy rumbled.

Mother Hen came back in and popped the onions into the pan. Then she had another taste.

"Turnips!" she decided. "While I dig some up, just chop me some wood, would you?"

"OK," said the Big Bad Wolf. "But I need my dinner. SOON."

"Nearly ready," smiled Mother Hen. "Just polish the silver while I add some cabbage and potatoes."

"OK," said the Big Bad Wolf. "But HURRY UP!"

"READY!" shouted Mother Hen, stirring in some mushrooms and cheese.

Wolf tucked his napkin into his collar and took a huge mouthful of soup.

"DEEELICIOUS!" he declared. "The best soup I've ever tasted. Who'd have thought that a stone could make such DEEELICIOUS soup."

"Have some more," said Mother Hen.

The Big Bad Wolf ate and ate and ate until all the soup had gone.

"Now," sighed Mother Hen, "you can eat me."

"Oh no," gasped the Wolf, "I couldn't eat another mouthful."

"Oh dear," said Mother Hen, "then you had better run off with all my lovely things. But please, *please*, don't take my soup stone."

The Big Bad Wolf leapt up with a crafty smile on his face, grabbed the stone and ran from the house as fast as he could.

And Mother Hen? She leant back in her chair and laughed and laughed and laughed until the tears ran down her face.

All
Creatures
Great and
Small

The Three Billy Goats Gruff

There were once three billy goats, who were called the Billy Goats Gruff.

They lived on a hill, which had once been covered in thick green grass. But the goats had eaten it all, and since it was a very hot dry summer, no new grass grew and the three Billy Goats Gruff got thinner and thinner.

Now just across a little stream, the goats could see a field. This field was still full of thick green grass and every time that they looked at it, they felt their tummies rumble.

You might wonder why they didn't just walk over the little bridge to the thick green grass. I'll tell you why. It was because a wicked old troll, with eyes as big as saucers and a nose as long as a poker, lived under the bridge and he liked nothing better than gobbling up goats.

Eventually the goats grew so hungry that they decided, troll or no troll, they must go over the bridge to the field of thick green grass.

The smallest Billy Goat Gruff went first, trip-trap, trip-trap, over the rickety rackety bridge.

"WHO'S THAT TRIP-TRAPPING OVER MY RICKETY RACKETY BRIDGE?" roared the troll.

"It's only me, the teeniest tiniest Billy Goat Gruff, going to the field for some thick green grass. Please let me pass," squeaked the smallest billy goat.

"No," growled the troll. "I'm going to gobble you up. Yum, yum."

"Please don't gobble me up," pleaded the smallest billy goat. "Wait until the second Billy Goat Gruff comes, he's MUCH bigger than me."

"Oh, all right then," said the greedy old troll and the smallest Billy Goat Gruff skipped off into the thick green grass and started munching.

The middle-sized Billy Goat Gruff went second, trip-trap, trip-trap over the rickety rackety bridge.

"WHO'S THAT TRIP-TRAPPING OVER MY RICKETY RACKETY BRIDGE?" roared the troll.

"It's only me, the slightly bigger than tiny Billy Goat Gruff, going to the field for some thick green grass. Please let me pass," said the middle-sized Billy Goat Gruff in the tiniest voice that he had.

"No," growled the troll. "I'm going to gobble you up. Yum, yum."

"Please don't gobble me up," pleaded the middle-sized billy goat. "Wait until big Billy Goat Gruff comes, he's much bigger than me."

"Oh, all right then," said the greedy old troll. And middle-sized Billy Goat Gruff cantered off into the thick green grass and started munching.

Big Billy Goat Gruff went third, trip-trap, trip-trap, over the rickety rackety bridge.

"WHO'S THAT TRIP-TRAPPING OVER MY RICKETY RACKETY BRIDGE?" roared the troll.

"IT'S ME, the great BIG Billy Goat Gruff, going to the field for some thick green grass," roared back the great big Billy Goat Gruff.

"Oh, no you're not," shouted the greedy old troll, "because I am going to gobble you up. Yum, yum."

"Come on then," shouted great big Billy Goat Gruff. But when the troll clambered onto the bridge, the great BIG Billy Goat Gruff hooked his horns through the seat of the troll's trousers and swung him round and round, then he tossed him into the air.

And the wicked old troll, with eyes as big as saucers and a nose as long as a poker, whizzed up and up and up into the sky.

And for all I know, he might have landed on the sun or the moon, because nobody ever saw him again, and the three Billy Goats Gruff ate up all the thick green grass. So:

Snip, snap, snout,

This tale's told out!

The Three Little Piggies

Mrs Pig's three little piggies ate SO much that Mrs Pig said, "Time to build your own homes, my lovely little piggie wiggies. Then I can come to visit and have tea with you."

So off went the three little piggies, dreaming of the lovely houses that each of them would build. They hadn't gone far down the road when they met a goat with a cart full of straw.

"Please, Mister Goat," said the teeny weeny piggy, "may I PLEASE have some straw to build a house?"

"Certainly," said the goat, "and when you have built your house I will come and have tea with you."

So the teeny weeny piggy began to build a beautiful house of straw. Off went the other two little piggies, dreaming of the lovely houses that each of them would build. They hadn't gone far down the road when they met a dog with a cartload of sticks.

"Please, Mister Dog," said the middle piggy, "may I PLEASE have some sticks to build a house?"

"Certainly," said the dog, "and when you have built your house I will come and have tea with you."

So the middle piggy began to build a beautiful house of sticks.

Off went the biggest piggy dreaming of the lovely house that she would build. She hadn't gone far down the road when she met a cat with a cartload of bricks.

"Please, Mister Cat," said the biggest piggy, "may I PLEASE have some bricks to build a house?"

"Certainly," said the cat, "and when you have built your house I will come and have tea with you."

So the biggest piggy began to build a beautiful house of bricks.

Teeny weeny piggy's house was soon finished and he put on the kettle and popped a cake in the oven.

Suddenly, he heard a knock on his door and a deep growly voice said: "Little pig, little pig, let me come in."

"No, no, no! By the hairs on my chinny chin chin, I will NOT let you in," squeaked the teeny weeny piggy, trembling from head to toe.

"Then," said the Big Bad Wolf, "I'll huff and I'll puff and I'll BLOW your house down!"

So he huffed and he puffed and he blew down the beautiful little straw house. But the straw floated up his nose and he sat down, sneezing and sneezing so the teeny weeny piggy grabbed his cake and ran and ran until he arrived at his brother's house of sticks.

"Hello, middle piggy," he called. "I've brought a cake for tea."

Middle piggy put on the kettle in his beautiful house of sticks and sliced up some sandwiches. Suddenly, there was a knock on his door and a deep growly, sneezy voice said: "Little pig, little pig, let me come in."

"No, no, no! By the hairs on my chinny chin chin, I will NOT let you in," squealed middle piggy, as his knees loudly knocked together.

"Then," said the Big Bad Wolf, "I'll huff and I'll puff and I'll BLOW your house down."

So he huffed and he puffed and he blew down the beautiful house of sticks.

Most of the sticks fell on his head and as he struggled to get up, teeny weeny piggy grabbed his cake and middle piggy grabbed his sandwiches and they ran and ran until they arrived at their big sister's house of bricks.

"Hello, biggest piggy," they shouted. "We've brought cake and sandwiches for tea."

Biggest piggy put on the kettle in her beautiful house of bricks and stoked up the fire. "We'll toast some crumpets too," she said.

Suddenly, they heard a knock at the door. "Little pigs, little pigs, let me come in."

"No, no, by the hairs on our chinny chin chins, we will NOT let you in," shrieked all three little piggies.

80

"Then I'll huff and I'll puff and I'll BLOW your house down," roared the Big Bad Wolf.

So he huffed and he puffed and he huffed and he puffed and he HUFFED and he PUFFED, but . . . he could not blow down the house of bricks!

The wolf was very angry AND very hungry too. He had expected to have eaten not one, not two, but THREE little piggies by now.

"I know what I'll do," thought the wolf. "I'll climb down their chimney and gobble them up."

So he climbed up onto the roof and started to slide down the chimney. But the little piggies heard him coming and stoked the fire even higher, and when that wolf's bottom touched the flames, he HOWLED and SHOT up the chimney, higher and higher into the sky.

And from that day onward, that Big Bad Wolf NEVER bothered the three little piggies again. And they held lovely tea parties every afternoon.

The Hare and the Tortoise

Hare was a very fast runner and a great big show-off. Tortoise was very slow and quiet.

One day Hare was showing off more than usual, turning somersaults and back-flips and shouting: "I'm so clever. I can turn back-flips and cartwheels. I can jump as high as the moon and I can run as fast as the wind, no one can beat me!"

Tortoise was so fed up with Hare's boasting, and before he knew what he was doing, he shouted back: "You're just a great big show-off. I bet that I can run just as fast as you."

As soon as the words were out, Tortoise knew he had made a mistake. Everyone was staring at him.

"All right then," said Hare. "Prove it! We'll have a race. Right now!"

"Right NOW?" gulped Tortoise.

"Right now," said Hare. "Let's get ready."

Fox and Pig marked out the track and stood with a piece of string at the finishing line.

"Ready," shouted cat.

"Steady," shouted bat.

"GO!" shouted rat.

Hare ran like the wind and when he looked over his shoulder, Tortoise was nowhere to be seen.

So he slowed down, then he stopped. Finding some nice dandelions to eat he sat down in the sun and nibbled at their petals.

His eyelids felt heavy. "Just a little snooze," he thought. "Tortoise is so slow that I have plenty of time for a little nap."

When he woke up again, the sun was just setting and in the distance he heard a lot of noise, music and shouting. He leaped up and he ran like the wind to the finishing line.

But, oh no! Tortoise was already there!

"You are fast," said Tortoise to Hare. "But you are not so clever."

"Tortoise is the champion!" cheered the other animals, hoisting him up on their shoulders.

Hare slunk away feeling very foolish. And never again did he boast that he could not be beaten.

The Gingerbread Man

There was once a little boy whose very favourite food was gingerbread. One day, his mum popped a gingerbread man into the oven and said to her son, "I'm just taking your dad some sandwiches and a drink. He'll be hungry and thirsty after working in the fields all morning. Will you keep an eye on your gingerbread man and make sure that he doesn't burn?"

No sooner had his mum gone out, than the oven door burst open and out jumped the gingerbread man. He looked at the little boy and ran away laughing:

> *"Run, run, as fast as you can,*
> *you can't catch me,*
> *I'm the gingerbread man."*

The little boy ran after him shouting and yelling and when he ran past the field where his dad was working, his mum and dad both joined the chase.

Next the gingerbread man passed a black and white cow.

"Mmmm," mooed the cow. "Please stop. You look tasty and I want to eat you!"

But the gingerbread man ran even faster, shouting:

"I've run away from the little boy, I've run away from his mum and dad. I'll run away from you too!

"Run, run, as fast as you can, you can't catch me, I'm the gingerbread man."

The cow ran as fast as she could, but that wasn't VERY fast, because she needed milking.

Next the gingerbread man passed a big dappled horse.

"Mmmm," neighed the horse. "Please stop. You look tasty and I want to eat you."

But the gingerbread man ran even faster, shouting:

"I've run away from the little boy, I've run away from his mum and dad, I've run away from the black and white cow and I'll run away from you too!

"Run, run, as fast as you can, you can't catch me, I'm the gingerbread man."

The horse galloped as fast as he could but the gingerbread man went faster.

He raced on and on until he came to a river and had to stop.

By the river sat a fox.

"Hello, little gingerbread man," smiled the fox. "Do you want to cross the river?"

"Ooh yes I do!" said the gingerbread man.

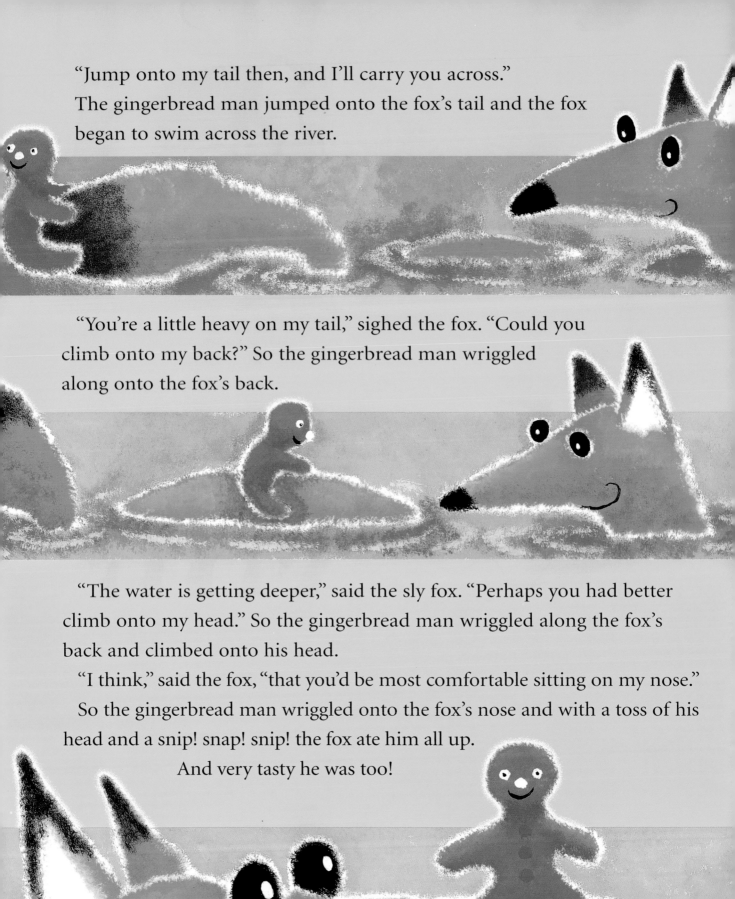

"Jump onto my tail then, and I'll carry you across."
The gingerbread man jumped onto the fox's tail and the fox
began to swim across the river.

"You're a little heavy on my tail," sighed the fox. "Could you
climb onto my back?" So the gingerbread man wriggled
along onto the fox's back.

"The water is getting deeper," said the sly fox. "Perhaps you had better
climb onto my head." So the gingerbread man wriggled along the fox's
back and climbed onto his head.

"I think," said the fox, "that you'd be most comfortable sitting on my nose."
So the gingerbread man wriggled onto the fox's nose and with a toss of his
head and a snip! snap! snip! the fox ate him all up.

And very tasty he was too!

Brer Anancy and Brer Tiger

Once upon a time there lived a
creature who was half man and
half spider and his name was Brer
Anancy. Now there was nothing
in the world Brer Anancy wanted
more than to have his own stories.

But at that time the only creature
who had his own stories was Brer Tiger.

One day Brer Anancy asked Brer Tiger if he could change
the name of Brer Tiger stories to Brer Anancy stories.

But Brer Tiger loved having the stories
about himself so he said, "NO!"

"Please, please, please," begged Brer Anancy. "I'll do anything you wish."

"OK," said Brer Tiger. "If you can catch a bottle of live bees and then catch a live snake and a live monkey, I will let my stories be called Brer Anancy stories."

Brer Tiger was just teasing. He was sure that Brer Anancy would not be able to do these three things. But Brer Anancy went away thinking very hard.

The next day Brer Anancy walked towards a beehive holding a jar. He walked slowly and said loudly, "How many will it hold?"

Soon he saw the Queen Bee and said even more loudly, "How many will it hold?"

The Queen Bee was curious. "What do you want to know, Brer Anancy?" she asked.

"Well," said Brer Anancy. "Brer Tiger thinks that this jar will hold twenty bees and I think that it will hold fifty bees."

"Let's find out," said the Queen Bee and she called the bees from the hive to climb into the jar.

When it was full, Brer Anancy put on the lid and ran back to Brer Tiger.

Brer Tiger was furious, but he was sure that Brer Anancy could not catch a live snake and a live monkey. But Brer Anancy went away thinking very hard.

The next day Brer Anancy cut a very long piece of bamboo and walked to where he knew that he would find Brer Snake.

As he walked past, Brer Snake called out, "Where are you taking that little stick, Brer Anancy?"

"This isn't a little stick, it's a very long stick," replied Brer Anancy. "I bet that it's longer than you are."

"Nonsense," said Brer Snake. "Lay it on the ground and I shall lie next to it, then we shall see who is longest."

So Brer Anancy laid the stick on the ground and Brer Snake lay next to it.

"You fidget so, Brer Snake," sighed Brer Anancy. "How can I measure you against the stick when you fidget so? Let me tie you to the stick so that you are still."

"OK," said Brer Snake, sure that he was
the longest. But as soon as he was tied
to the stick, Brer Anancy took him
to show to Brer Tiger.

Brer Tiger was furious, but
he was sure that Brer Anancy
could not catch a live monkey.
But Brer Anancy went away
thinking very hard.

The next day Brer Anancy made a clay man and put some ripe bananas into the clay man's hand. He put the clay man on the path leading to Brer Monkey's house and hid behind a bush.

Soon greedy Brer Monkey came down the path. When he saw the bananas he said, "Give me those bananas!"

But the clay man said nothing. So naughty Brer Monkey hit the clay man with his right hand and it stuck fast in the clay. Then he hit the clay man with his left hand and that stuck fast in the clay too. Then Brer Monkey kicked the clay man, first with his right foot, then with his left foot and both of his feet stuck fast in the clay.

Then Brer Anancy jumped out from behind the bush, grabbed the clay man and Brer Monkey – who was stuck fast – and ran back to Brer Tiger.

Brer Tiger was furious. He did not want to lose his stories, but he kept his promise. And that is how the Brer Anancy stories came to be.

Dwarves
and
Giants

Jack and the Beanstalk

There was once a little boy called Jack who lived with his mother. They were very poor and one day his mother said, "Jack, you must take our cow to market and sell her, for we have no money left."

Jack set off to market and he had not gone very far when he met a funny little man.

"Hello, Jack," said the funny little man. "Where are you going this fine day?"

"To sell my cow," answered Jack.

The little man pulled a bag out of his pocket and emptied seven brightly coloured beans onto the palm of his hand. They were the most beautiful beans that Jack had ever seen.

"I will give you my seven magic beans in exchange for your cow," said the little old man.

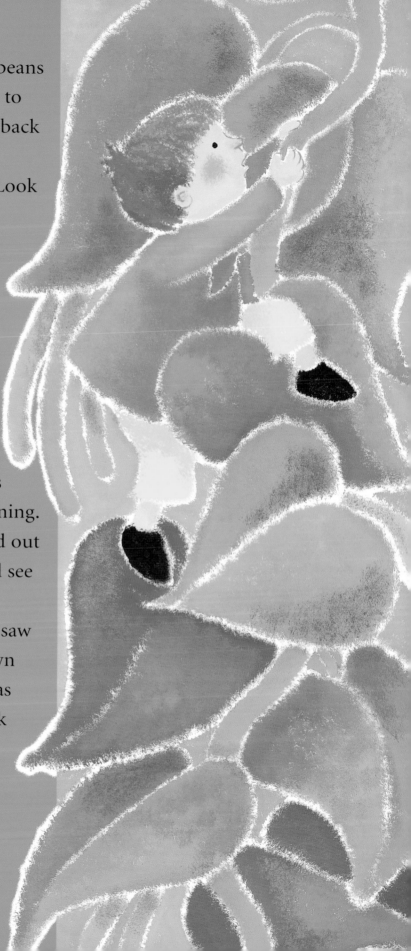

Jack wanted those beautiful beans very much, so he gave the cow to the funny little man and went back home with his bag of beans.

"Look, Mother!" he called. "Look at my beautiful beans."

"You sold our cow for seven beans, you silly boy!" she replied, astonished, and she burst into tears and threw the beans out of the window.

That night they went to bed hungry. Jack was so hungry that the grumbling noise his tummy made woke him just as the sun came up the next morning.

He got out of bed and looked out of his window, but all he could see was huge green leaves.

He ran out of the house and saw that one of the beans had grown overnight. It had leaves as big as dustbin lids and a stem as thick as four elephants' legs and it disappeared into the clouds.

Jack just had to climb it. Up and up he went, and up and up again.

Just as he felt too tired to go any further, he reached the top and found himself in a magical place. There was a huge castle in front of him and Jack knocked on the door.

It was opened by an enormous lady.

"Please," said Jack, "I'm tired and so very hungry. Will you give me something to eat and a chair to sit down in for a while?"

The enormous lady looked worried. "This castle belongs to a wicked giant," she said, "and if he finds you here he will eat you all up."

Just then the floor and walls started shaking.

"Ooooo! That's him coming home now!" cried the lady, and she hid Jack in the teapot.

"Fee, fie, foe, foy, I can smell . . . a little boy!" shouted the giant.

"Nonsense," said the enormous lady. "It's the smell of your stew simmering on the stove."

Jack listened to the giant. He was really fierce. He shouted at the enormous lady and tried to hit her with his big stick, but she moved too fast for him.

When he had eaten his
dinner, he told her to bring
him his hen.

It was a beautiful golden
hen and when the giant
said, "Lay me an egg," the
hen laid an egg, and then
another and another until
there was a whole basketful.

Then the giant fell asleep.
At once Jack crept out of the
teapot, tucked the hen under
his arm, and climbed back
down the beanstalk.

The next day Jack and his
mum had eggs for breakfast
and then Jack's mother went
off to market with two huge
baskets of eggs to sell.

As soon as she had gone,
Jack climbed back up the
beanstalk and knocked at the
castle door. Once again, the
enormous lady opened it.
"You shouldn't have come
back," she wailed. "If he
catches you he'll eat you
all up."

Just then the floor and the walls of the castle started shaking.

"Quick!" cried the enormous lady. "He's coming home." And she hid Jack in the sugar bowl.

"Fee, fie, foe, foy. I can smell . . . a little boy!" shouted the giant.

"Nonsense," said the enormous lady. "It's just your sausages sizzling on the stove."

The giant was even more horrible to the enormous lady than he had been the night before. He tried to trip her up when she served his sausages, he complained about the food, and he put out his tongue at her behind her back.

When he had finished his dinner, he told the enormous lady to bring
him his sacks of gold and his magic harp.

The giant counted his gold as the magic harp played beautiful music and
soon he nodded off to sleep.

As soon as he was fast asleep, Jack climbed out of the sugar bowl and
hoisted the sacks of gold onto his back. He picked up the harp, but the
harp was magic and started shouting, "Help me, help me, I'm being stolen."

Jack ran as fast as he could, but the giant woke up and started to run
after him.

The enormous lady tripped
the giant right over, but
he got up again and
followed Jack to the magic-
bean plant and started
to follow him down.
Jack moved faster
than he had ever done
in his life and when he reached
the bottom of the beanstalk,
he grabbed an axe from
a pile of firewood and
started to chop down the
beanstalk. No sooner had
he struck the first blow,
than there was a blinding blue
flash and the magic plant and
the giant disappeared for ever.

Jack and his mum now had
enough money to live happily
and that's just what they did
for the rest of their lives.

And so did the enormous
lady, because when the giant
disappeared, she was left with
the castle to herself, and no
wicked giant to boss her about.

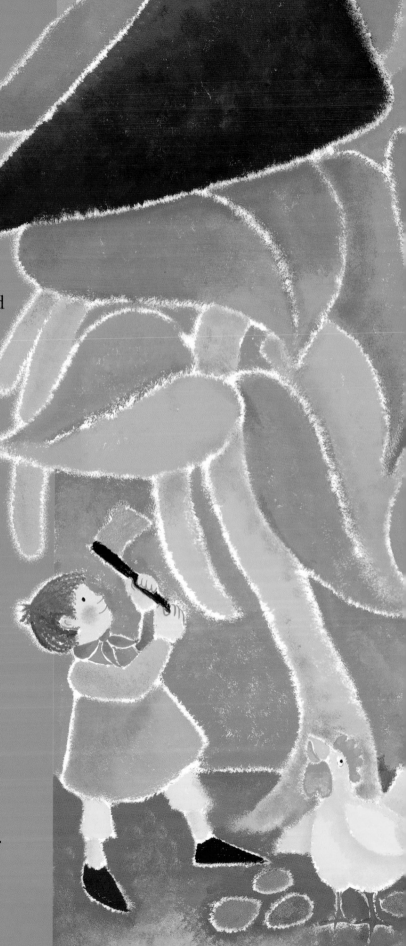

110

Puss in Boots

There was once a young man, who found himself all alone in the world with only his cat for company.

"Oh dear," he sighed, "how are me and my puss going to live when I have no home and just one piece of gold left in the whole wide world?"

To his surprise, his cat spoke up. "Spend your last gold piece on a fine pair of boots for me and give me a large sack, and I will help you to make your fortune."

The young man was so astonished to find that his cat could speak, he had no trouble at all in believing what he said. He gave him a big sack and then straight away he went to the bootmaker and ordered the most splendid pair of boots.

The cat was so
pleased with them
that he wore
them all the
time and that's
how he got his name
– Puss in Boots.

One day Puss put
on his boots and
took his sack into
the woods. There
he caught two
plump rabbits. Into
his sack they went
and Puss set off for
the king's palace.

When he arrived, he demanded to see the king at once. The people at the palace were so amazed to see a cat wearing boots, and one who could speak as well as they could, that they took him straight to the king.

"Your majesty," said Puss, bowing low, "I bring you a gift of rabbits from my master, the Marquis of Carabas!"

Puss had just made up the name for his young master – clever Puss!

The king was very pleased with his rabbits and told Puss to thank his master.

The next day Puss brought the king two pheasants, and while he was at the palace, he heard that the king was planning to go riding in his carriage with his beautiful daughter that very afternoon.

Puss ran back to his master as fast as he could.

"Do as I tell you, master," gasped Puss, "and your fortune is made. Trust me!"

The young man did trust Puss and when Puss said he should take off all his clothes and jump into the river he did as he was told. Just then the king's coach came into sight.

Puss ran up the riverbank shouting, "Help, oh help! My master, the Marquis of Carabas, is drowning. Thieves set upon him, stole his clothes, and threw him in the river."

Immediately the king sent two of his men to rescue the Marquis of Carabas and two others to fetch him some new clothes.

Once the young man was dressed in fine clothes, he looked very handsome indeed, and the princess could not help looking at him.

Puss was delighted and ran off ahead. He soon came to some huge green meadows. "Whose meadows are these?" he asked an old man.

"They belong to a wicked ogre, who makes our lives totally miserable," said the old man.

"When the king passes and asks whose meadows they are, tell him that they belong to the Marquis of Carabas," said Puss. "If you do this, I promise to help with your problem."

So when the king passed in his coach and asked, "Whose meadows are these?" the old man answered just as Puss had wanted him to.

Next Puss came to some vast fields of golden wheat. He asked an old woman about the owner and he got the same answer: the fields were owned by a wicked ogre. Again Puss promised to help the old woman with her problem, if she told the king that the fields belonged to the Marquis of Carabas. So when the king came by in his coach, she answered his question just as Puss wanted her to.

Finally Puss came to a beautiful castle and knocked on the door.

The door was opened by an enormous ogre, who eyed Puss greedily.

Puss kept his distance as he bowed and asked, "Are you the mighty ogre, who can turn himself into any large animal that he wishes to?"

"Yes, I am he!" boomed the ogre.

"What, even a lion?" asked Puss. "Surely you can't do that!"
In a flash the ogre became a huge roaring lion. Puss kept well out of his way.

When the lion had turned back into an ogre again, Puss said, "I bet that turning yourself into something *small* is much more difficult. I bet for instance that you can't turn yourself into a mouse."

"EASY!" roared the ogre and instantly, there in front of Puss sat a tiny mouse, which straight away Puss pounced on and gobbled up.

When the king knocked on the castle door, it was opened by Puss, who bowed low and said, "Welcome to the castle of my master, the Marquis of Carabas."

The young man was nearly as astonished as the king at the splendour of his new home. Before they left the castle the king suggested that since his daughter had so obviously fallen in love with the Marquis of Carabas, perhaps they should get married!

There was great rejoicing all round. The ogre was gone, so Puss had kept his promise to the people who had helped him, and he had kept his promise to his master.

The marquis and the princess lived happily ever after. And so did Puss in Boots.

Rumpelstiltskin

There was once a miller who had a very beautiful daughter. She was so beautiful that soon the king got to hear of her.

The king called the miller to his palace to ask him about his daughter. Now the miller was a very silly man. He thought that it wasn't enough to be both beautiful and clever, so he boasted to the king. "My daughter is not only beautiful, and as bright as a button," he said, "but she can . . . she can . . . SHE CAN SPIN STRAW INTO GOLD!"

The king was amazed. "Bring her to the palace at once," he ordered. "And if you are telling the truth, she shall become my wife."

The miller took his poor daughter to the palace and that night the king took her to a room full of straw and said, "Spin this straw into gold by the morning and prove that your father was not lying."

And he locked the door behind him. Of course the poor girl had no idea how to spin straw into gold and she began to cry.

Just then she heard a voice. Standing in front of her was a tiny little man.

"Why do you cry, miller's daughter?" he squeaked.

"Because I have to spin this straw into gold by morning, and I have no idea how to do it," she sobbed.

"What will you give me to do it for you?"

"My necklace," said the miller's daughter and Bish-bosh! the straw was turned into gold in the twinkling of an eye.

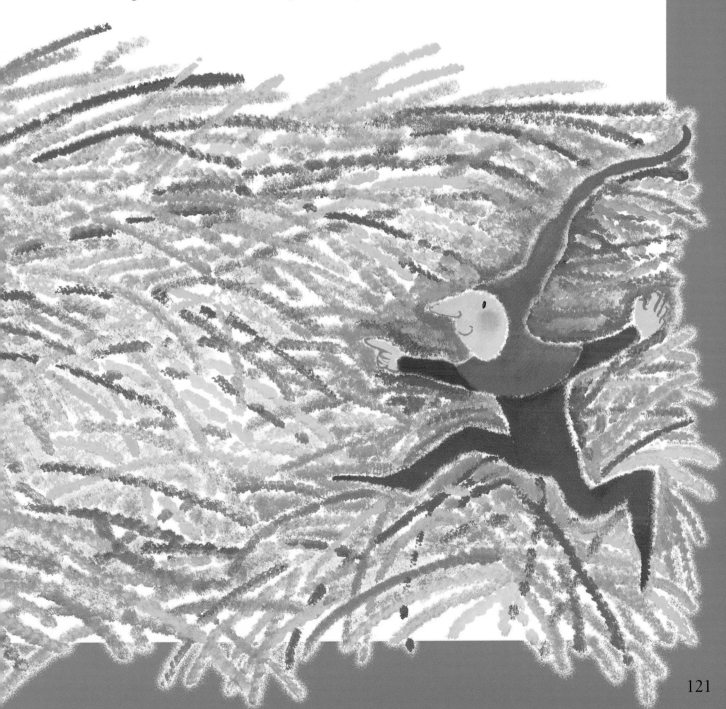

When the king unlocked the door the following morning, he was very pleased.

"Wonderful!" he cried. "Tonight you can spin me twice as much gold!"

That night, he shut the poor miller's daughter into an even bigger room full of straw.

Once again the little man appeared.

"What will you give me if I spin this straw into gold?" he squeaked.

"My ring," said the miller's daughter and Bish-bosh! the straw was turned to gold in the twinkling of an eye.

When the king unlocked the door the following morning, he was very, very pleased.

"Wonderful," he cried. "Now you can spin me three times as much gold, and if you do this, I shall marry you, and you'll never have to spin again."

As soon as she was alone the little man appeared again.

"What will you give me if I spin this straw into gold?" he squeaked.

"Alas, I have nothing left to give," wailed the miller's daughter.

"Then promise me your first child when you are queen," he squeaked.

The poor miller's daughter thought hard. Why, that might never happen, she thought, so she agreed.

The king was thrilled with his gold and kept his promise. They were married the next day and a year later the queen gave birth to a beautiful baby boy.

She was so happy with her baby
that she had quite forgotten her
promise to the little man.

But one day he came to her room
and demanded that she give
him her baby prince.

She offered gold, jewels, half the kingdom, but he would not budge. The
poor queen started to cry and, feeling just a little sorry for her, the tiny
man said, "You may keep your baby if you can guess my name. You have
three days in which to do it. I'll be back to see you tomorrow night."

The queen spent the whole night writing lists of all the names she knew
and the next morning sent a messenger out to gather all the names that he
could find.

The following night when the little man arrived, she asked, "Is your
name Nick or Dick or Rick? Is it Leo or Rio or Theo?"

"No it is not!" shouted the little man.

The following night she asked him silly names. "Is it Bottom or Sausage-
nose or Poggy Doggy?"

"No it is not!" shouted the little man.

On the third day the messenger returned late in the evening.
"I have no new names," he said, "but late last night, as I climbed into the high, high mountains, where the hare and the fox say goodnight to each other, I saw a tiny man dancing round a fire singing:

'Burn fire burn   Tomorrow the prince
For they'll never learn   Will be my kin
My name,   Because my name
What a shame!   Is RUMPELSTILTSKIN!'"

The queen jumped for joy and when
the little man came in she asked, "Is your
name John?"

"No it is not!"

"Is it Tom?"

"NO it is not!"

"THEN . . . it must be
RUMPELSTILTSKIN!"

The little man flew into a fury.
"A witch must have told you!"
he screamed.

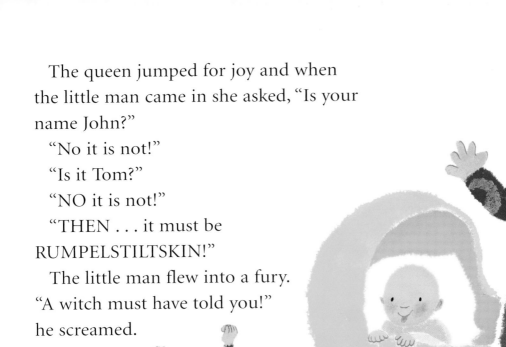

And he stamped his feet so hard that,
to the queen's astonishment, he
disappeared right through the floor.
And he was never seen again.

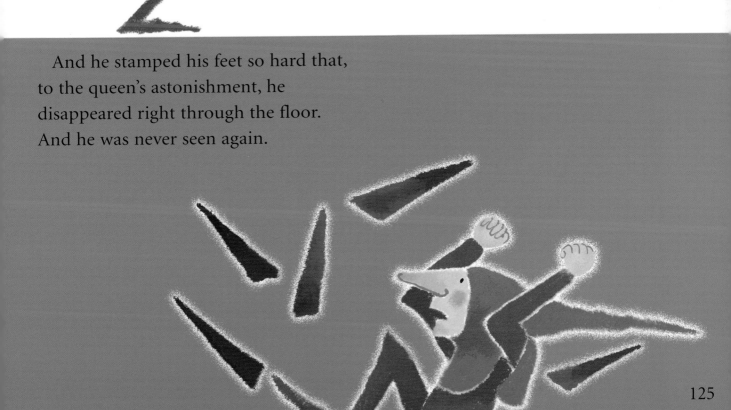

The Selfish Giant

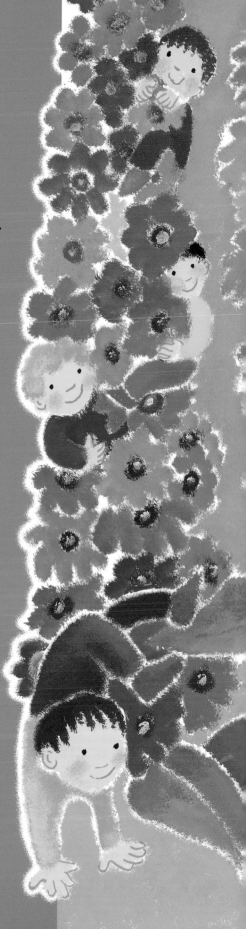

There was once a most beautiful garden. In the garden was a house and in that house lived a giant.

Every afternoon he went to visit another giant, and every afternoon after school the children ran into his garden to play.

One day the giant came back early. When he saw the children playing in his beautiful garden, he was furious. "Go away, you naughty, naughty children," he shouted. "It is my garden, not yours. You will spoil it!"

So he built a high wall around his beautiful garden and the children no longer came in to play.

He was a very selfish giant!

Winter passed and spring came. All the trees began to blossom and the flowers pushed their way up through the bare earth. But in the giant's garden the snow still lay deep. The giant longed for the spring, but the months went by and still the snow lay as deep as ever.

One morning, the giant was woken by a beautiful sound. It was a bird singing. He looked out of his window and saw that the snow was melting. Through a little hole in the wall, the children were creeping. They were climbing the trees and as they touched the branches the trees burst into blossom.

The giant hurried
down to the garden,
but when the children
saw him coming,
they were frightened
and hid away.

   All except for one.
One little boy stood
crying by a snowy tree.
He was too small to
reach even the
lowest branches.

   Gently the giant lifted
him into the tree.
As he touched it,
the snow melted
and the blossom
began to bloom.

"How selfish I have been," said the giant. "It is the children who bring life and laughter into my garden. It is the children who make it beautiful."

And he took a great axe and knocked down the wall.

When the children saw how the giant had changed, they came out of their hiding places and from that day on, the garden became their own. The giant played with the children in what had become the most beautiful garden in the world.

Fairy
Land

Sleeping Beauty

Once there were a king and queen, who wanted a baby more than anything else in the world. One day their wish came true and they had a beautiful baby girl.

They were so happy that they decided to have a huge party for her christening. They invited all their friends and relations and all the fairies in the kingdom, except for one. This was because nobody knew where she lived and nobody had seen her for years and years.

The party was wonderful. Everybody ate and drank and laughed and sang. As it was drawing to its end, the fairies stood up and began to offer the baby wonderful gifts, in fact everything that you could possibly wish for. Just as the last fairy bent to offer her gift, the palace doors burst open and in came the most furious fairy that you've ever seen.

She would listen to none of the king and queen's apologies for not inviting her. She stormed up to the baby's cradle and raised her wand.

"Make the most of your gifts," she shrieked, "because when you are fifteen, you will prick your finger on a spinning wheel and DIE!"

And without another word she disappeared in a puff of purple smoke.

Everybody began to weep and wail but the youngest fairy, who had not yet given her gift, stepped forward. "I cannot undo that spell," she said, "but I can alter it. The princess will not die. Instead she will sleep for one hundred years."

The king was sure that he could stop the wicked fairy's curse from coming true, so he had all of the spinning wheels in the kingdom destroyed.

The princess grew up into a beautiful, clever, kind and happy girl. Her fifteenth birthday came and went and her father felt sure that all would be well.

One day as she played in the palace, the princess discovered a tower that she had never seen before. She climbed the stairs and in the room at the top she found an old woman sitting at a spinning wheel.

The princess stepped into the room and asked the old woman what she was doing.

"Spinning," she answered. "Come and have a try."

No sooner had she touched the spinning wheel than the princess pricked her finger and fell into a deep sleep.

At that moment everyone else in the palace also fell asleep.
The king, the queen, the courtiers, the cook, the kitchen maids,
even the horses in their stables and the doves on the roof.

Years went by and a huge hedge of roses grew around the palace so that it could no longer be seen. Soon people forgot that the palace was there. Just a very few old people seemed to remember that a princess slept beyond the tumble of flowers.

One day a young prince rode through the country and spied the hedge of roses. As he rode towards it the bushes parted and let him pass through. You see, a hundred years had passed and it was time for the princess to wake up.

He rode up to the palace and stared in amazement at the sleeping people and animals.

He walked through the palace, past the king and queen asleep on their thrones and up the stairs to where the princess lay.

She looked so lovely and so peaceful that he just had to stoop and kiss her. Immediately, she opened her eyes and slowly smiled at him.

Hand in hand, they walked down to the king and queen, who wept with delight to see their daughter again. And it won't surprise you to hear that the prince and princess were soon married and lived happily together for the rest of their lives.

The Elves and the Shoemaker

There was once a shoemaker – and very nice shoes he made too – but somehow he never seemed to earn enough money.

The day came when he only had enough leather left to make one last pair of shoes. Carefully he cut out the pattern and arranged the pieces on his bench ready to sew the following morning. Then he went sadly off to bed.

The next day when he went down to his workroom, he couldn't believe his eyes. There, on the bench where he had left the pieces of leather, was the most beautiful pair of shoes!

He picked them up in wonder. They were made with such tiny stitches that you could hardly see the sewing at all. And with the little pieces of leather that had been left over, delicate flowers had been made to decorate the shoes.

The shoemaker put them in his window and immediately his shop filled with people pushing and shoving each other as they offered more and more money for the lovely shoes.

The shoemaker soon had enough money to buy leather to make *two* pairs of shoes. Again he cut out the pieces and left them on his bench ready to sew the next morning.

When he got up the following day, he found, once again, that the sewing had been done for him! There on his bench were two delicately stitched pairs of shoes. Once again, they sold as soon as he put them in the window.

Now the shoemaker had enough money to buy leather for *four* pairs of shoes.

So it went on for weeks and weeks. Now the shoemaker could buy the very best leather and suede and silks and velvets and brocades and lovely trimmings for his shoes. The townspeople paid him a lot of money for the beautiful shoes and soon he became very rich.

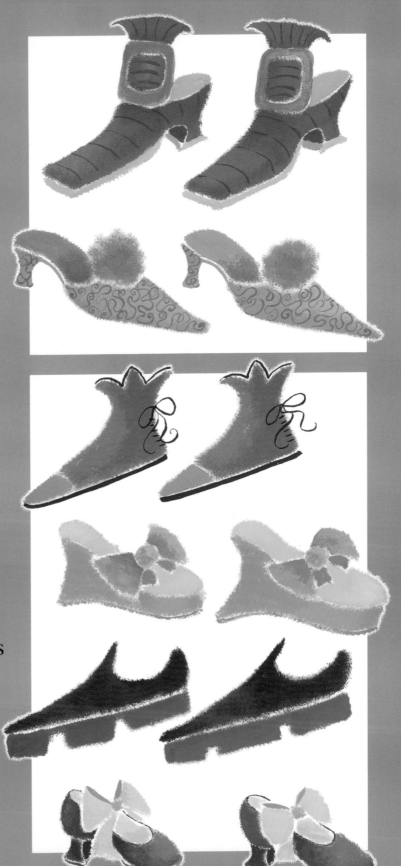

Now the shoemaker was a kind and generous man, and he
wanted to share his good fortune with his secret helpers.
One night, the shoemaker and his wife crept downstairs and
peeped into the workshop.

There, sitting on his bench were two tiny elves, with not a
stitch of clothing on, sewing away at his shoes and singing
as they worked.

When the shoes were finished, they disappeared, POP!
just like that.

The next day, the shoemaker and his wife sat down and sewed two lovely sets of clothes: little shirts and trousers and waistcoats, scarves and hats and overcoats and tiny scarlet leather boots.

That night, the shoemaker and his wife tiptoed downstairs once more and peeped into the workshop where they had laid out the little clothes.

On the stroke of midnight, the elves appeared. They shrieked with delight at the sight of the clothes. Quickly they put them on.

Laughing and singing they danced around the room and skipped out into the street and were never seen again.

But the shoemaker found that from that day on the shoes that he made were every bit as beautiful as the ones the elves had sewn. And he and his wife lived comfortably for the rest of their days.

The Woman who Flummoxed the Fairies

There was once a woman who baked cakes. Her cakes were so delicious that she became known as the best baker for miles around.

She baked cakes for every wedding and christening, for rich and poor alike. She was also a good-hearted woman and she gave her cakes away to those who had no money.

She was not only a
wonderful baker; she
was also very clever. One
day her baking got her
into trouble, but her
cleverness got her out of it!
I'll tell you what happened.

More than anything else, fairies
like a bit of cake. They will creep
into people's kitchens at night, and
help themselves to a little slice.

There were some fairies who
lived in a hill near to the
wonderful baker. Alas, her cakes
were so good that there was
never a crumb left over for them.
So they decided to carry the
woman away to fairyland to
bake cakes for them alone.

One night as she was
walking home from a
hard day spent baking
hundreds of cakes in the
king's kitchen, the fairies,
who had been hiding
near the fairy mound,
flew out and dropped
fern seeds into her eyes.

Immediately she felt sleepy and lay down to rest on the fairy mound.

She fell deeply asleep, and when she woke up she found herself . . . in fairyland!

"Well, well," she said, "I've always wanted to visit fairyland and here I am."

The fairies told her that they were going to keep her there for ever and always, just to bake cakes for them.

"Very well," she said cheerfully, "let's get started."

She opened her bag, took out a clean apron and then looked around.

Oh dear. The fairies had nothing for her to bake with. So she sent them to her cottage. Some for eggs, some for sugar, some for flour, some for butter. Back they came with their tiny arms full.

But, oh dear. The fairies' own mixing bowl was the size of a tiny tea cup. So she sent them back to her cottage. Some for a bowl, some for wooden spoons, some for an egg whisk. Soon the fairies were tired out from flying.

The woman began to measure and mix and whisk and beat.

Then she stopped.

"Oh dear," she sighed. "I can't mix without my cat purring next to me."

So off the fairies went to fetch her cat.

The woman stirred away at her bowl.

Then she stopped.

"Oh dear," she sighed. "I can't mix without my dog snoring at my side."

So off went the
fairies to fetch
her dog.

The woman beat
her batter again.

Then she
stopped.

"Oh dear,"
she sighed. "I'm
so worried about
my baby at home
teething that I just
can't mix."

So off went the
fairies to fetch
her baby.

When he
arrived he was
very hungry and
started to scream.

"Oh dear,"
sighed the
woman. "If my
husband were
here, he could
quieten the baby."

So off the fairies went to fetch her husband. When her husband arrived, she winked at him and handed the baby a wooden spoon. The baby banged and screamed and banged and screamed.

"Pinch the dog," whispered the woman to her husband.

"Bow wow wow, bow wow wow," barked the dog.

"Bang, scream, bang, scream!" went the baby.

"Tread on the cat's tail," whispered the woman to her husband.

"MEEOW, MEEOW," howled the cat.

"BOW WOW WOW, BOW WOW WOW," barked the dog.

"SCREAM, BANG. SCREAM, BANG," went the baby.

The fairies
didn't know what
to do. They flew
around with
their hands over
their ears. You
see, fairies hate
loud noises more
than anything,
and the woman
knew it.

When the cake mix was ready, the woman put it into two tins, popped a sugar lump into the baby's mouth and winked at her husband.

At once he stopped pinching the dog and treading on the cat's tail and all became quiet. The fairies slumped down exhausted.

"Right," said the woman, "where's the oven?"

Oh dear. The fairies had no oven.

"NO OVEN!" gasped the woman. "How can I bake your cake without an oven?"

There was nothing for it. The exhausted fairies had to let the woman and her household
go back to the
cottage.

"But you will have your cake," promised the woman. When she got home, she baked the cake in her oven, and when it was cool, she took it to the fairy mound. There she found a bag of gold in payment.

After that she baked a cake for the fairies every week, and every week they left a bag of gold for her. Soon she was not only the best baker in the county, but the richest too!

And they all lived, as they deserved to do, happily ever after.

Princes and Princesses

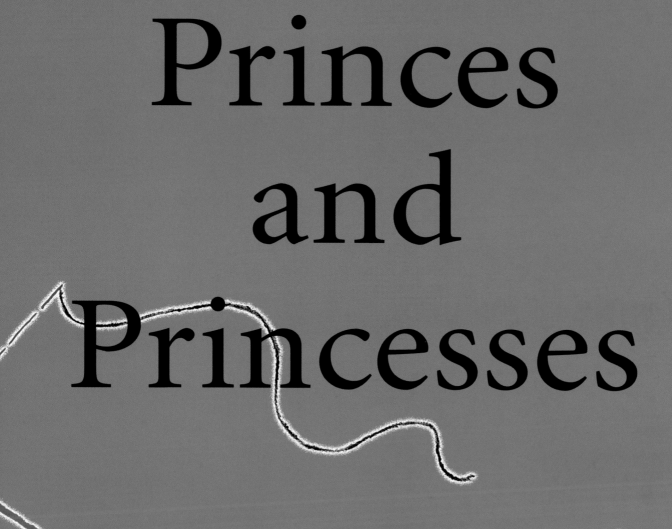

The Frog Prince

There was once a beautiful princess who liked nothing better than playing with her golden ball. One very hot day, she went to play in the shade of the trees by the old water well. Being too hot to run about, she sat on the edge of the well, tossing her ball into the air and catching it.

Maybe she grew careless or maybe a little magic happened, because when she tossed the ball into the air, it dropped, NOT into her hands, but into the deep dark well. The princess began to cry because the golden ball was her favourite toy. Suddenly she heard a voice close by. There, on the edge of the well, sat a fat green frog.

"Why are you crying, Princess?" he asked.

"Because, stupid frog, my beautiful golden ball has fallen into the well," she replied rudely.

"I'll get it for you," croaked the frog. "But only if you promise to be my friend and play with me and eat with me and let me sleep on your pillow."

"All right," said the princess.

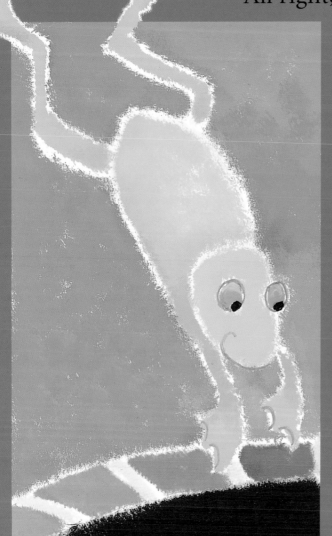
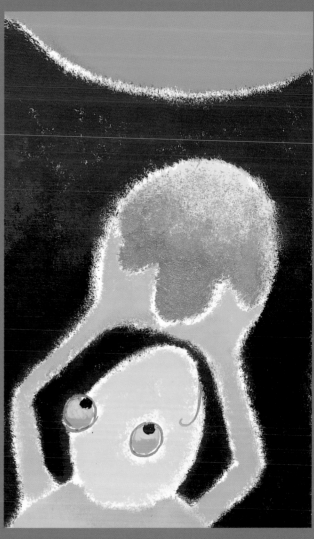

So the frog dived into the well and brought the princess back her ball.

Without even saying thank you, she snatched it up and ran back to the palace as fast as she could; leaving the poor frog wailing, "Wait for me!"

That evening as she was eating her supper, she heard
a plip-plop, plip-plop sound on the stairs and then a
knock on the dining room door.

"Princess, Princess, let me in," croaked a froggy voice.

But the princess pretended that she could not hear it.

"Who is that calling for you, my daughter?"
asked the king.

So the princess told him the story
of the frog, the ball
and the well.

"Well then," said the king. "A promise is a promise, my dear. Open the door at once and let the frog in."

The princess was very angry, but in came the frog. He jumped on the table and began to eat off her plate. How she hated it!

When it was bedtime the frog followed her up to her room. First he washed in her bowl and then he snuggled down on her pillow. The princess lay as far from him as she possibly could.

When she woke the next morning, the frog had gone. "Goody," she thought. But next evening there came the same plip-plop sound on the stairs followed by a knock on the door. The frog was back! This time the princess felt that she knew him a little better and was not so unkind. By the third night, she was quite looking forward to his company and they carried on talking to each other in bed even after the candles were snuffed out.

In the morning the frog hopped off her pillow but when he landed on the floor, he turned into a handsome prince.

"Thank you, Princess," he said. "Because you became my friend, you broke the spell that a wicked fairy had put on me. She turned me into a frog, and a frog I had to stay until somebody truly became my friend."

The handsome prince asked the princess to marry him, to which she readily agreed.

At once a beautiful coach with eight fine horses appeared and carried them off to the prince's kingdom, where they lived happily ever after.

The Princess and the Pea

There was once a prince, handsome of course, who wanted to marry a princess, beautiful of course. But, even more important, she had to be a truly REAL princess.

He went off travelling all over the world, where he met many princesses, but he could never be quite sure that they were REAL princesses.

At first glance they seemed to be, but then there was always something that did not seem quite right.

So he came back home again, looking very miserable. He had so wanted to meet a REAL princess and marry her.

One night, soon after he had returned, there was a most terrible storm.

FLASH! went the lightning.

CRASH! went the thunder.

And the rain made rivers of the roads.

In the middle of this storm, there was a loud knocking on the palace door and the king himself went to see who was there.

Outside stood a princess, but oh dear what a sorry sight she was. Her clothes were sodden, her hair was plastered to her head, rain dripped off the end of her nose and squelched over the top of her shoes. "I may look wretched," she said, "but I am a REAL princess!"

Hmm, thought the queen, we'll soon see about that. And without saying a word, she hurried off to the spare room. She took all the bedclothes from the bed and put a pea on the mattress. Then she put twenty more mattresses on top of it and twenty feather eiderdowns on top of them.

The princess had a hot bath and was then shown to her bedroom.

The next morning the queen asked how she had slept.

"Alas," replied the princess, "despite all those mattresses and eiderdowns, I barely slept a wink. There must have been something huge and hard in the bed. Look, I'm black and blue all over! It was horrible."

"Hurrah!" cried the queen.

"Yippee!" yelled the prince.

"Wonderful!" warbled the king.

"She's a truly REAL princess."

They, of course, knew that only a REAL princess would have skin so soft she could feel a pea through twenty mattresses and twenty eiderdowns.

So the prince married her and the pea was placed on a silken cushion, in a glass case, in the museum, where you can see it still, unless someone has stolen it!

And this is a true story, REALLY.

The Twelve Dancing Princesses

There was once a king who had twelve beautiful daughters.

They all slept together in one huge room and every night, as soon as they were tucked up in bed, the king locked their door with a big golden key.

Each morning, he would unlock
the door and there, beside
their beds, were their
dancing slippers,
all danced to rags
and tatters.

The king had no idea how this could happen and he grew more and
more worried as he saw his beautiful daughters become pale, worn out
and thinner every day.

So the king let it be known that if anyone could find where his
daughters went each night, he would reward him. First, by letting him
marry the princess of his choice, and then by crowning him king.

Many young princes came to try their luck. They would eat their dinner with the princesses, and then be taken to a room next to the princesses' bedroom so that they could keep watch, and find out where the twelve princesses went to dance their shoes to rags and tatters.

But none of these young men had any luck. No sooner did they go to their room, than they fell fast asleep, and when they awoke in the morning, the princesses were back in their beds, pale and worn out, with their shoes danced to rags and tatters.

The king became more and more worried.

One day, as a poor young man called Tom was walking towards the king's castle, he met an old woman. When she asked him where he was going, Tom said that he wouldn't mind finding out where the twelve princesses went to dance, so that he could become king.

The old woman smiled kindly at Tom. "Here is a gift for you," she said. "Put on this cloak which will make you invisible. Then you can follow the twelve princesses to where they dance their shoes to rags and tatters. But be sure not to drink the wine set out for you when you go to your room, for it will send you into a deep sleep."

Tom arrived at the palace and was made as welcome as all the princes had been. He dined with the twelve beautiful princesses and then was taken to his room. When no one was looking, he tipped away his wine and lay down and snored as if he were sound asleep.

As soon as the princesses heard his snores, they slipped on their shoes and tapped once on the eldest princess's bed. At once it sank through the floor and beneath it was a flight of stairs. Down they all went, one after the other.

Immediately, Tom put on his cloak and crept after them. Halfway down the stairs, he trod on the hem of the youngest princess's frock. "Who's pulling my dress!" she cried. "Silly," said her eldest sister; "you've just caught it on a nail."

At the bottom of
the stairs was a
beautiful avenue
of silver trees.
The leaves tinkled
in the breeze and
Tom snapped off
a leaf and hid it
in his pocket.

"What's that
noise?" cried the
youngest princess.

"It's fireworks,"
said her eldest
sister, "to welcome
us to the dance."

They came to a
second avenue,
where all the trees
were gold, and a
third where they
were all diamonds.
In both avenues,
Tom broke off
a leaf and hid
it in his pocket.

Each time the
youngest princess
gasped, "What's
that noise?"

And each time
her eldest sister
replied, "It's only
fireworks, silly!"

Next they came to a vast lake with a beautiful castle in the middle. The twelve princesses climbed into twelve little boats lit with lanterns and sailed across the lake.

Tom hopped into the youngest princess's boat.

"My boat is going slower than all of yours," she cried to her sisters.

"There must be a big old fish hanging on behind," laughed her eldest sister.

When they arrived at the castle, music filled the air. The princesses could not resist the bewitching sound and their feet began to dance.

They danced faster and faster until they stumbled, exhausted, with their shoes danced to rags and tatters, back across the lake and up the secret stairs to their bedroom.

Tom ran ahead of them up the steps and jumped into his bed and started snoring loudly.

"You see?" said the eldest princess. "Nothing to worry about, he's fast asleep."

The next morning the king called Tom to him and asked him a question.

"Young man, where do my twelve beautiful daughters go to at night, and dance their shoes to rags and tatters?"

Tom answered, "They go down avenues of silver, gold and diamonds, to a lake which they sail across, to a castle where they dance, until they drop with exhaustion."

And he pulled the silver, gold and diamond leaves from his pocket to prove it.

And with that the spell was broken and the twelve princesses soon became strong and healthy again.

And Tom? He married the youngest princess
and became a good and wise king.

Magic

Cinderella

There was once a man who married for the second time. His new wife was absolutely horrible! She had two daughters, who were just as horrible as their mother.

Now this man already had a little daughter, but his new wife and her two daughters were jealous of her and as soon as they arrived they began to make her life as miserable as they could.

Her dad was often away from home, and when he was gone his little daughter was made to do all the cleaning and washing and cooking.

In the evening she would crawl among the cinders in the chimney corner to try to keep warm. Because of this, her stepmother called her Cinderella. But even though she was not happy, she was a kind girl and got on with her work as best she could.

One day a letter arrived from the prince, inviting any young ladies in the family to a grand ball at the palace.

Cinderella's two stepsisters were thrilled and they called Cinderella to help them get ready. They spent hours trying on different dresses in front of the mirror.

Then the sisters said, "Cinderella, would you like to go to the ball too?" but they were only teasing and when Cinderella said yes, they just laughed and said, "What, you! You go to the palace in your cindery rags and tatters! You must be joking!"

After they had gone
poor Cinderella
just sat down
and cried.
But suddenly to her
amazement her
godmother appeared.
Now Cinderella's
godmother was no
ordinary godmother.
She was a fairy and she
was determined that
Cinderella should go
to the ball.
"Now just dry those
tears and fetch me the
biggest pumpkin that
you can find," she said.
Cinderella fetched
the pumpkin and
her godmother
struck it with
her magic
wand.

197

BAZAM! At once the pumpkin became a golden coach. Next her godmother asked for the mouse trap. Inside were four little grey mice. BEZAZZ! She waved her wand and the mice became four pretty dapple-grey horses.

Then she asked Cinderella to bring her a large black rat.
ZWOOSH! The rat became a jolly coach driver with curling whiskers.
Last of all she asked Cinderella to fetch her four lizards from the garden.
WHEEEEEE! The four lizards became four
fine footmen who jumped up on the back
of the coach.

But still Cinderella cried, "It's all so wonderful, but I can't go to the ball wearing these rags."

Her godmother touched Cinderella with her wand and immediately she was dressed in the most beautiful ball gown and on her tiny feet were twinkling glass slippers.

Her fairy godmother sent her off with a word of warning.

"On the stroke of midnight, the magic stops. Make sure that you leave the ball in time to get safely home again."

As soon as she arrived at the ball, the prince went up to her and took her hand. She was so lovely, he danced with her all evening. They were so busy dancing and laughing and talking that, too late, Cinderella heard the palace clock begin to strike midnight.

She ran like the wind down the palace steps, losing one of her little glass slippers as she raced towards her coach.

She leapt in and the coach sped out of the palace gates. Suddenly Cinderella found herself sitting on a pumpkin in her ragged clothes, surrounded by mice, lizards and a rat!

She only just reached home before her sisters. They told her about the beautiful stranger who seemed to have won the prince's heart.

Indeed they were right. The following day the prince announced that whoever's foot fitted the little glass slipper, which he had found on the palace steps, would become his wife.

All the young ladies in the kingdom tried on the shoe, but it fitted none of them. Eventually the shoe was brought to Cinderella's house for her two sisters to try. One sister curled her toes up tight and *nearly* wedged it onto her foot, but WHEE! it pinged off and hit the footman on his nose! The other sister pushed and shoved and ouched and eeked and tried to hide her huge heel that hung over the back of the slipper. But it was no use trying, the slipper just did NOT fit.

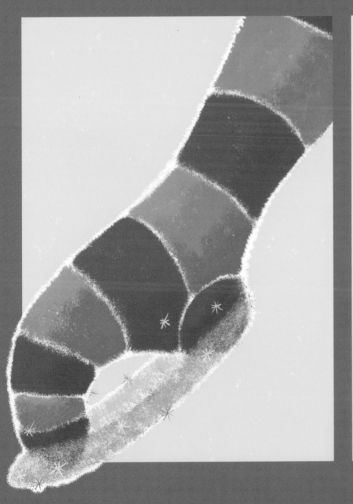
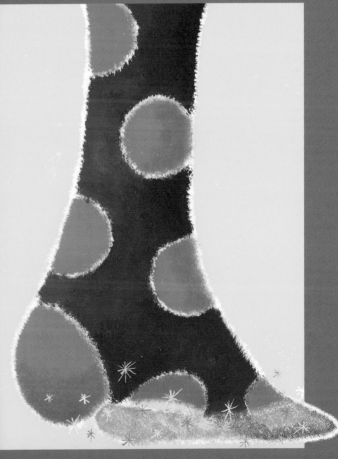

"Let me try," asked Cinderella, coming out of the kitchen.

"Don't be silly," said her sisters, "you're only a kitchen girl. You didn't even go to the ball."

But the footman said, "EVERY young lady in the kingdom must try it on."

Of course the slipper fitted perfectly and Cinderella pulled the other one from its hiding place and put it on.

The prince was overjoyed to find his true love and they were married soon afterwards. And do you know? Cinderella was so kind that she even found rich husbands for her two horrible sisters. But believe it or not, they were not in the least bit grateful.

The Magic Pasta Pot

Young Lucia lived with her mum on the edge of a little wood. They had very little money and often went hungry. One day Lucia went into the wood to pick some berries to eat, but she couldn't find any at all. She sat down on a tree stump and started to cry.

Just then she heard a voice. She looked up and saw a little old lady wearing a huge cloak.

"Don't cry, young Lucia," said the old lady kindly. "I have a present for you."

And from under her cloak she pulled a shiny copper pot.

"Put this pot on your stove and say, 'Boil, little pot,' and it will make you perfect pasta.

"When you have eaten enough, say, 'Stop, little pot,' and it will do as you ask."

Lucia hugged the little old woman and ran home as fast as she could.

She put the pot onto the stove and said, "Boil, little pot," and the pot made the most delicious macaroni for Lucia and her mother.

Each day the pot made every kind of pasta and delicious sauce that you could imagine and Lucia and her mum never went hungry.

Then it happened one day, when Lucia was out, that her mother wanted some pasta. So she put the pot onto the stove and cried, "Boil, little pot!" The pot made her the best spaghetti that she had ever tasted. When she had eaten enough, she said, "Thank you, little pot, you can stop now."

But the little pot *didn't* stop. More and more spaghetti appeared until it reached the top of the pot and started to wiggle over the sides.

Lucia's mum jumped back. "No more, no more!" she cried. "I've had enough!"

But the pot carried on cooking the pasta and soon
it was snaking across the floor. Lucia's mum ran out of
the door and down the path towards the village.
   The pot boiled faster and faster. Spaghetti wriggled
down the path after her.

It coiled and swirled its way down every village street. Just then Lucia came round the corner and met the squiggling, wiggling mass of spaghetti.

She knew at once what to do: she gathered as many villagers as she could, and told them to scream, "STOP, LITTLE POT!" all together and at once. And they did just that, at the top of their voices.

At last, the little pot stopped.

That day, the villagers had the biggest pasta party that you could ever imagine, and what was left was soon gobbled up by the cats and dogs.

After that young Lucia took charge of the pot and once a year she and her mother invited everyone to the village square for a wonderful pasta party.

The Three Wishes

There was once a poor fisherman. One day when he was out fishing, he felt something very heavy in his net. He heaved and he tugged until the net broke the surface of the water, and there, all tangled up, was the largest and oddest fish that he had ever set eyes on. Indeed it was an odd fish, because it could speak as well!

"Please don't eat me," begged the fish. "I am a magic fish and if you promise to throw me back in, I will grant you three wishes. Also," he added, "magic fish really do taste horrible."

So the fisherman agreed to throw him back in exchange for the three wishes.

He hurried home to tell his wife the good news and they decided to think very carefully about what they should wish for. His wife found a bottle of wine left over from last Christmas and they poured a glass each to celebrate their good luck.

The fisherman had his first sip of wine and without thinking at all, he sighed and said, "I wish that we had a big juicy sausage to eat with this wine."

No sooner had he said this, than a huge sausage
plopped down his chimney and flopped across
the floor and up onto the table. His wife
stared in horror.

"You STUPID husband!" she shouted. "We've been given three wishes and you've just wasted one on a *sausage*. You're a silly daft idiot. If you had wished to be rich we could have bought as many sausages as we liked."

"I'm sorry," said the fisher-man. "I wasn't thinking."

"Sorry!" screamed his wife. "Sorry's not good enough. I'll give you sorry!" And she started chasing the poor fisherman round the room, trying to hit him with the sausage.

"I wish that sausage would stick to your nose," shouted the fisherman.

Oh dear. No sooner had he said this than the huge sausage stuck onto his wife's nose and every time she tried to shout, the sausage bobbed into her mouth and she couldn't say a word.

The fisherman stared at his wife in horror. He felt really sorry for her, because although he had been very angry with her, he really did love her.

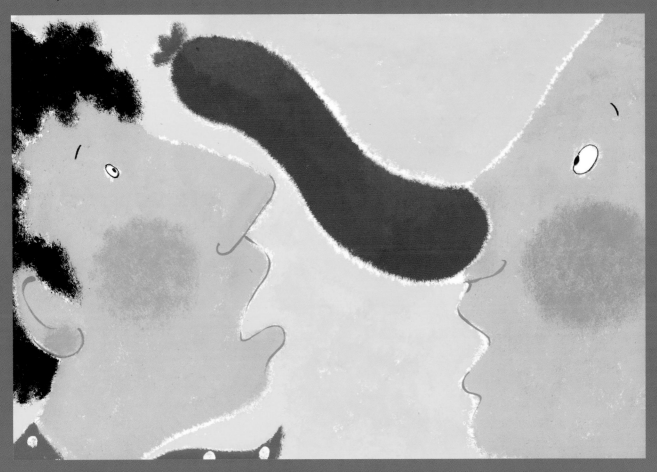

So what could he do? His wife could not go through the whole of her life with a great big sausage on her nose! So he had no choice but to use his last wish to get rid of that wretched sausage. And, do you know, they not only wasted their three wishes, but they didn't even get to eat the sausage.

Index